How Deep the Sharpened Blade

How Deep the Sharpened Blade

A Pulp Collection from the Wood Shed Writers

Edited by Beverlee Blair
Designed by Meghan Snatchko
Photographs by Meghan Snatchko,
except where noted.

Published by Wood Shed Writers
348 Maplewood Ave
Ambridge, PA 15003
www.woodshedwriters.com

ISBN: 979-8-9958616-0-7

TABLE OF CONTENTS

INTRODUCTION
BEVERLEE BLAIR
EDITOR

The world that I grew up in reeked of stories. A house full of people and music, books and games, a working-class neighborhood that ebbed and flowed, stories told, unspoken, hidden in the air around me, under my feet, beckoning, repelling, murmured in semi-darkness. Writing has been a constant in a kaleidoscopic life. Never a good retirement plan, it has nevertheless been the only game in town. Through my youth in a haunted, small town; buoying my escape to live outside and hone my craft. Through college and liberal arts, through dance with the miraculous Consuelo Atlas, acting classes on a dare, from *Life on the Water* whose opening act was Spaulding Grey to an investigations agency whose clients were on death row, through the hell of ruined lives and finding a way out to get back home. From shedding the Pigpen aura of horror and sorrow, pen in hand, to teaching a creative writing class at a small-town arts center, refocused and energized.

Wood Shed Writers started small. Voices telling stories grew from a whisper to an oxymoronically melodic shriek. Only those with game—those who were game—rose to the challenge of no word limit pulp, a genre with the broadest possible range and depth. And here we are with our first pulp collection. Black and white and read, please, all over.

- B

UNFURLED
BY HOLLY THYEN

The lonely young woman had learned to steer clear of the ocean on calm, sunny days. Even though she longed to feel the cool waters of the Mediterranean Sea lapping between her toes, she heard the snakes hissing every time she approached the tidal pools near the shoreline. When she first arrived upon the island, she often wondered if it was her presence near the waters that stirred them up.

Recently, Medusa had begun staying up on the cliffs near the rocky ledge to gaze down upon the expanse of cerulean blue in front of her. She often stood for hours as she tried her best not to flinch. Medusa hoped the snakes would take their cue from her and remain still without getting stirred up. Standing sentry on the ledge of a cliff reminded her of her younger days, not so long ago, when she was a maiden in the temple overlooking the same shimmering waters from a different, far away land.

She remembered on one occasion being frightened by large brown and green speckled snakes when she was a newly ordained priestess in Athena's temple. The snakes were thrown onto the marble steps by warriors and slithered toward the inner sanctuary. She immediately turned to run into the temple when she noticed the older priestesses laughing at her frightened reaction. They were jealous of her youthful beauty. Unlike the snakes surrounding her now, the javelin sand boas did not have poisonous bites. Later, she learned the snakes had been sent by Ares as a vindictive means of attempting to annoy and irritate Athena, his half-sister.

She had given up on the belief that anyone was coming to save her. When she first arrived upon the island, she held out a fractal of hope the size of a grain of sand that some sort of hero would wash up on the shore and turn out to be her savior. She even prayed to the gods who had betrayed her. Now her only companions were the snakes she often feared. She worried that she would have to charm them in order to protect herself from being infected, or perhaps even killed, by their venom. She closed her eyes, held her chin up high, and felt the wind rush over her face. The snakes were quiet now. She could barely hear them hissing.

The snakes provided a warning alarm when strange vessels appeared upon the horizon. They would intuitively sense the presence of strangers approaching the island and hiss in unison, creating a frequency that vibrated her sternum. This often occurred when she napped in the verdant wildflower area a few meters back from the top of the cliffs.

In the late afternoon, she turned from the cliff and made her way to that soft, lush spot where she often rested. It wasn't long before the rays of the beaming sun and the sweet, intoxicating smell of jasmine lulled her to sleep amongst the tall grasses. She felt safer settling into sleep away from any view of the sea. Napping far from the water staved off the nightmare of Poseidon's assault on her in the temple. The god of the ocean had attacked without warning, leaving her physically and emotionally torn apart on the marble floor of the temple. When Athena heard what had happened in her temple, she reacted by blaming Medusa. Athena then cursed Medusa by taking away her beauty and banishing her to a far away island. Then Athena crowned Medusa's head with venomous reptiles.

Now, as Medusa slept, the snakes stretched themselves out to bathe in the sun's warmth, forming a crown around her head resembling the one worn by Apollo. Suddenly, she was awakened by a pulling sensation on her temple followed by a chorus of hissing. She bolted upright and turned her head toward the sea. The snakes unfurled themselves, separated from each other, and lifted their heads up high. She felt them pulling on all sides of her head. She noticed that she could feel the warmth of the sun on the back of her neck as she slowly made her way forward. In her peripheral vision, she could see the snakes' red slitted tongues glinting in the late afternoon sun.

Medusa knew that while she napped the snakes sensed that someone was approaching. She stood up and walked toward the cliffs overlooking the shore. The snakes kept their long necks upright and their heads held high.

She knew the snakes could feel the vibrations of human footsteps and could strike out in response. She scanned the horizon and didn't see any outlines of a pentaconter in the sea. She leaned over and glanced down toward the caves. There were no footprints in the sand. The snakes started bobbing their heads up and down as the wind picked up. They stretched their heads forward and away from her temple as they pulled at her scalp. She realized the snakes had caught a whiff of someone or something new and potentially dangerous in the wind.

Medusa turned her back to the setting sun and began to run toward the entrance to the cave she called home. She decided that she would hide there until the imminent danger had passed. Suddenly, she felt the nest of snakes pull toward the sky as a shadow crossed overhead, momentarily blocking out the late afternoon sun. She glanced up and saw a quick flash of a creature flying by toward the ledges of the cliff overlooking the beach. She wondered if it was an eagle that had noticed the swaying snakes attached to her head. She feared it would soon circle back around in order to take a swipe at one of them. However, as the shadow passed over her again, she didn't see a distinct figure with outstretched wings. Instead, when she looked up at it, she was momentarily blinded by a sharp bright light shining directly into her eyes. The snakes hissed and ducked down toward her shoulders. Quickly, she ran toward one of the stone figures of men that dotted the landscape near her cave. She darted around to the side of the figure that was facing the

4

entrance to it. She stooped down low in order to make herself as small as possible. Her face pressed close onto the granite folds of the statue's tunic.

However, the snakes betrayed her. They refused to make themselves small. They continued to stretch and pull in order to get a better idea of who this new trespasser was. They pulled so hard they forced her to look up. The first thing she noticed was the tortured look on the face of the petrified statue that was giving her refuge. The former young sailor had huge wide eyes and a gaping mouth.

In a flash, Medusa remembered hearing the screams of young men when she ran out of the cave the morning they came to her island. The snakes had been particularly restless all night. A few had lunged toward a critter that had crawled into the cave, jolting her awake. She had finally dozed off again at the break of dawn when early morning rays of sun stretched into the cave's entrance, lulling the snakes to sleep despite their

restlessness. Then, all of a sudden, she heard the men's voices. They sounded like they were laughing and making fun of each other.

Due to the fog of lack of sleep, she had almost forgotten about the curse. For a split second, she thought the men were there to save her. She ran out of the cave to a chorus of hisses. One snake reached around so far forward that she thought it might try to bite her on the cheek. She called out to the men, who appeared to be exploring the island and foraging for food.

They looked up in unison when they heard her voice, and immediately thereafter began to scream in horror.

Medusa stopped in her tracks. The men had ceased moving at all and were staring at her. She had thought that her curse was to live forever in isolation, but she had not fully understood the extent to which her appearance would frighten and then destroy men. She knew then in an instant why the snakes forbade her from walking near the tidal pools on the beach. They wanted to prevent her from seeing her reflection.

Right before the men screamed, Medusa entertained the fleeting thought that Athena had changed her mind and taken pity upon her by reversing the curse. She then watched in horror as the men tried to turn to flee from her but were stuck in place. Their sandaled feet turned to stone. Granite began to creep its way up from the men's calves to their hips and waists. Their screams turned to wails and grew even louder. Instinctively, she rushed toward them. When the stone spread to their throats, the screaming stopped. She observed that their eyes had grown so wide they looked as if they were going to explode out of their heads. Within a few seconds after that, the island was silent again except for the sound of the wind rustling through the grasses and the waves crashing against the rocks on the beach.

Now, Medusa crouched behind the stone remnant of a once vibrant young man. His eyes were frozen open the moment she had unwittingly scared him to death. Suddenly, she noticed the wingless shadow circling overhead. She crouched further down in order to hide her entire body within the confines of the stone sailor's afternoon shadow. She glanced up in the sky to see the outline of a young man dressed as a warrior with winged sandals flying overhead. When he turned around to face the granite soldier graveyard, she noticed the Aegis shield he carried in his hand. It reflected the sun's harsh rays back into her eyes. She knew the shield was the handiwork of Athena.

Medusa hung her head as the snakes surrounding it began to pull away and up into the air as if to force her up on her feet, like a puppeteer yanking on a puppet by its strings. It felt as if the snakes were willing her to stand up and fight. They pulled so hard she had to raise her head to look at the sky. Instead, she saw her reflection in the mirror overhead. It reflected back to her an image of a vibrant wildflower garden infiltrated with grey statues of men in various positions of retreat. Their faces were etched in fear. Behind one frozen, hunched over statue of a man with bent knees and outstretched arms crouched a figure of a woman with hideous features and a nest of snakes upon her head. They were slithering and stretching away from her face as if they were preparing to strike.

Medusa knew she would never be forgiven for the crime she did not commit. She longed to escape from her cursed life. She quietly began humming to the snakes in order to charm them back into sleeping as she lay down in the grass behind the petrified soldier. The snakes stopped hissing and began to sway back and forth as their venom receded from their fangs and flowed back to the glands behind their eyes. As she put her head down, she felt the snakes' slithering slow down.

She closed her eyes and prayed the blow would come quickly, before the snakes could awaken. Only then would the curse be broken. She hoped her spirit would then fly free on the back of a white winged horse galloping through the sunlit sky. Then she would unfurl.

FADES AND BRIDGES
BY JASON BROWN

am an almost 40-year-old married man. My 12-year-old son wants to know why I am who I am. He wants to know where I came from and why the world looks so different through my eyes. I plan on teaching early what I learned late. The mistakes that he will make must not be my shortcomings, repeated.

I absolutely hate changing barbers and having to walk into a new establishment. After 10 years with the same barber and with my son by my side, I was on a mission to get us both fresh haircuts and some food. A Google search sent us to Tarentum from New Kensington. We looked for parking for our full-sized SUV. When we arrived, we were greeted and seated. Clippers and razors were already shaving insecurities and boosting pride at every station. We watched blessed hands delivering quality fades and tapers with crisp hairlines. The scent of Barbicide and isopropyl alcohol filled the shop, and the barbers all seemed to nod in sync with the bass line from vibrating speakers. The anxiety brought on by my having to trust new hands with sharp instruments gradually subsided as I watched the skillful shaping of styles so that men already seated in barber chairs began to see their reflections being shaped into the way they perceived themselves.

"Son, are you getting all of your hair cut off today?" I already knew the answer because there is so much of me in my son.

"No. I like my hair. I like the designs mom braids into it. I like my plaits, too. I'm just going to get my sides faded and everything shaped up."

This was safe and predictable. No quantum physics or mind-altering explanations needed. Then…

"Dad, why do you always grow your hair and cut it and why can't we just go to any barbershop?" And just like a dam or levy broke, and I was at the mercy of the current. "Dad, if your dad was in jail when you were my age, who took you to get a haircut? Oh, yeah, Dad, when did girls start liking your hair? Dad, was the barbershop close to your house like this is close to ours?" And since all we could do was hurry up and wait, I had to explain the layers of the life that I had lived and why I didn't want him to experience the 'hood'. "Dad, what three words would you use to describe yourself at my age? And what were you interested in?" I sat and tried to enjoy the ambiance of that place but I knew that honesty was the best policy. "Egocentric, independent and asinine, Son."

My path had taught me that a man is not rich until he had something that money could not buy. I knew that debt is a slave's currency. My teen years were spent in a neighborhood that valued respect and decency over money. Some households had less and some had more, but the fact that everyone was willing to share put paid to disparities. Most of the adults worked and

older kids looked after their younger siblings. Where I went, my younger brother went and if he couldn't go, then I couldn't go. Catching a PAT bus meant that I had to be more aware than ever because I never knew who or what I would be running into. My gear had to be fresh and I was not only a man, but *the* man. But nothing could have been further from the truth. I had the hand-me-downs from my uncles and cousins that were all still fast-money fresh. I spent so much time and effort being a label junkie when the 5-for-$20 Footlocker t-shirts were good heat in multiple flavors. I did whatever I could to scrape up money to buy my own clothes and shoes.

I started smoking marijuana but only when there were others around to see me smoking. I can only remember being high twice, which made me feel like the people smoking with me were only putting on a show. 'Vanity leads to insanity' is a lesson that took me way too long to understand. I had shoes stacked to the heavens and new, tagged clothes hanging on the pipe tapering the ceiling in the laundry room. I cared too much about outside validation. Some people fight their demons. I befriended mine and could not figure out that when you fuck up, you're falling down. I couldn't figure out why I still couldn't find the footing to stand in real life. Most people in my circle were there to see me fall, not to catch me the way I'd caught them. My quick-witted remarks got faster and my always 'kool' attitude got just a little bit frostier when I added jewelry to my repertoire.

We made our weekly trip to Willie T's in Homewood to get my hairline crisp and Nick's fade tight. I was officially out of my fade stage and into the crispy, even with sideburns that would never develop into a full beard. This barbershop was the heartbeat of Homewood, but we never had any problems. We weren't there for any static. Just haircuts, life lessons from the cutting edge of what was 'kool,' and honey barbecue wings from KFC on the other side of Frankstown. The coleslaw was wet and crisp, but not watery. Cornbread muffins and mean greens made us think somebody's big mamma was stashed in the back somewhere. This KFC was secured better than most bank vaults I've worked in as an adult. Bulletproof glass and turntable security doors for staff that had a magnetic and barge lock on it. Rumor had it there was a secret knock you had to do just to get in and start your shift.

I had Coogi, Durango boots, leather and suede butter Timberlands, Nikes, Jordans and Reeboks. Classics. Interchangeable parts that I never quite knew how to put together. Big brothers are usually good for teaching younger siblings how to blend styles and fashions. I picked up on cool music and in-style brands, and I knew that the barber by the window was the lookout for '5-0'. The barbershop was a one-stop shop for everything. Substance abuse paraprofessionals came in with household items, clothes…anything boost-able. I always assumed that most of the barbers sold weed or powder. The same as today. There was discretion, though, and kids like me were free to assume, but never knew exactly what the grown-ups were about.

"And, all this for what, Son? Absolutely nothing. I was trying to be seen when I should have been focusing on myself and my future. I can't fathom how much money and time I lost focusing on things that weren't important." Looking into the eyes of my legacy, I could see that he was absorbing all of the information and the stories he'd been given, but he was not at his saturation point yet.

The barber introduced himself as 'Shawn'. "I got an appointment that's more than five minutes late. I can squeeze one of y'all in."

Jason sat on the throne, ready for the king's treatment. I got to decompress. The clippers and scissors serenaded Jason's scalp and temples, and a more handsome version of me re-emerged. Perfect c-cups, an even fade and a line precise enough to make DaVinci blush. Google had done me right. A barber who has mastered his craft never rushes.

"Excuse me, sir. I have an opening for your haircut. Are you ready?" A different barber approached. I gave my phone and keys to my son and told him to think about someplace for us to eat.

FEBRUARY 1964
BY LISA MCCORMACK TAJAK

ROSE

CHAPTER ONE: HOG-TIED

"Oh Rose! You look lovely my dear." Mrs. Corso tugged at the hem of her dress and straightened the pillbox hat that tilted at a jaunty angle on Rose's brunette curls. "Only a few weeks left before that sister of yours ties the knot. You will be the perfect maid of honor."

"Thank you, Mrs. Corso. You've done wonders with taking in the waist. I really do appreciate everything, but I must be getting back to the office. Won't you be so kind as to pack up the dress and gloves? I'll be back to pick up the hat next week."

Rose looked at herself in the mirror one more time and with a wry smile assessed the horror of the pale green gown. The lighting in the dress shop made her skin look to be the same grim color, and it was all she could do not to burst into an anxious giggle. She quickly undressed and passed the gown through the changing room curtain to the waiting seamstress.

"I will pack this up straight away. Wouldn't want to keep Dr. Perlan waiting. God knows you keep that place running as smooth as silk. His wife was in the other day. A piece of work that one is," Mrs. Corso muttered, adding some other unflattering words as she packed the satin abomination into a garment bag to protect it from the drizzle outside.

Rose stepped out onto the sidewalk, coiling the dress securely around her arm as she opened her umbrella. Hardly anyone was out walking on Main Street this afternoon. The wind and the combination of light rain and snow seeped through her already damp trench coat. It was only two blocks to her office, and she was determined to resist the attempts of the fickle Pittsburgh weather to spoil her good mood. The Beatles were landing at JFK in New York right about now and would be on the Ed Sullivan show this Sunday. Rose smiled as she began almost to skip with excitement at the thought of watching the show on her grandmother's color TV!

Her pace slowed less than a block from the office when she noticed a hulking figure lowering himself into a dark Chevy Impala. Even through the slight fog Rose recognized the local thug, Marco Ricci. He looked up and noticed her, dismissing her with a smirk and ducking quickly into his car

"What's he doing here at this time of day?" she thought. "This isn't his usual neighborhood, nor the usual time of day that he does his kind of business." She felt uncertainty begin to well in her stomach and quickened her pace back to work.

The medical plaza was set back from the road on the corner of Main Street and the public parking lot. As Rose approached the office, she noticed that the frosted glass window on the door appeared dark from outside. The usual cool diffuse light from the waiting room fluorescents was absent. She struggled to push open the door as it caught on the snow mat wedged into the door frame.

Rose dropped her umbrella in a murky puddle outside and allowed the dress to crinkle carelessly in the crook of her arm as she pushed harder, forcing the door open far enough so she could slide her small frame into the waiting room. Rose flipped on the light switch by the door, looked into the room and stopped, frozen in place. As her arm fell limp to her side the garment bag fell into a heap at her feet. Laying on the waiting room floor was Dr. Perlan, naked except for his pale, yellow boxer shorts. He was hog-tied and gagged. A cut on his forehead bled onto the checkerboard tiled floor, but his eyes were wide open with fear; they were focused on Rose.

"Doctor…" Rose's voice shook as she stepped toward him.

Just then a loud crash from the nearby examination room interrupted her. Dr. Perlan shook his bloodied head and moaned an unintelligible warning. Rose lifted a gloved hand to her mouth and stifled a scream.

Once again, time froze and in that sudden silence the air seemed thick and unbreathable. Instinct took over as Rose crouched down and turned quickly back to the door. She slid her hand to the outside, grabbed her umbrella and pulled it toward her wrapping and snapping it tight. The makeshift weapon in her hand comforted her, reminding her of the wooden short-staff her Uncle Max had given her as a young girl. He had learned martial arts while stationed in Korea and taught her as a teenager.

Now she felt confident holding the umbrella above her head like a club. Heart pounding in her chest, she steadied her breath and padded toward the exam room like a predator focused on prey.

Rose peeked into the ransacked treatment room. Whoever had been there was now gone. She lowered the umbrella and noticed that the medical supply cabinet was turned over. Syringes, fresh gauze, and wooden tongue depressors lay mangled and twisted around broken glass jars. The window to the alley had been opened, and the chilly wind blew a wintry mix onto the rubble. Rose sidestepped the broken glass and pulled the window closed before hurrying back to tend to Dr. Perlan.

Kneeling on the floor, she began to remove the first aid tape and cloth medical masks the thieves had crammed into the doctor's mouth to quiet him. Rose tried not to gag as she removed the slimy cloth. He was soaked with sweat and coughed as his airway was cleared. Rose began to untie the cord binding his hands and feet. There were deep crimson indentations on his wrists from the pressure, and his fingers looked blue from the lack of circulation. Rose's strong and capable hands worked to free his arms and then his legs. He was shaking and as he tried to raise himself from the floor he seemed unsure of where to put his limbs for balance.

"What hurts?" she asked as she helped him to his feet and assessed the wounds on his forehead and wrists. In that moment, she felt grateful for the limited time she had spent in nursing school before she quit and came to work for Dr. Perlan. Yet it felt strange to ask her boss, the well-respected GP of their community, the question he had asked thousands of his patients over years. But here they were.

She helped him to his feet and held him steady as he tested out his legs, stumbling toward the mirror on the wall in the waiting room. He quickly surveyed his face, lifting a crimson-soaked white lock of hair from his forehead.

"It's a superficial laceration. I can take care of this myself." He then turned toward Rose. "I'm a bit banged up, but I don't think anything is broken." His face was crimped with uncertainty, and he said nothing more as he gingerly stepped toward the restroom.

Rose backed toward her desk, watching him. "I'm going to call the police!"

"No! Don't do that," Dr. Perlan commanded as he turned toward her. His face was pale and blood slid down his cheek and onto the floor.

"What?! Why not?" Rose was incredulous.

Dr. Perlan hesitated, weighing his options. "Rose, I'm not sure what to say. What happened today was a warning. Two thugs came in right after you left for lunch. Evidently their private doctor is getting old and sloppy. They need to find a new one— someone who would…ummm…cooperate?" Dr. Perlan raised his eyebrows as if questioning and dismissing her at the same time. He turned to walk back toward the restroom. She sensed he wasn't telling her the entire story.

Rose stood there for a moment, eyes widening with silent horror as she grasped the gravity of what had occurred in this office while she bantered with Mrs. Corso over weddings and ghastly dresses.

Dr. Perlan turned back, "Of course, I said 'no' and told them to leave. The bigger one grabbed my arm and said that he'd give me something to persuade me. He pulled out a pistol and hit me in the head with it. I must have passed out because when I woke up I was on the floor all tied up. They were looking down at me and the other one, the one who looked more like an accountant, warned me not to say anything and that they would be back for my answer."

"Rose," Dr. Perlan's voice was grave, "we can't call the police. I'm not sure what those men would do to me. To my family. To you. Did anyone see you come back to the office?" He looked toward the door as his voice tensed with new concern.

Rose looked down at the floor and noticed that the intruders had smashed the glass of the framed picture of the doctor's wife, Rita. Some of the doctor's blood formed a scarlet rose across her image. That wicked witch! "Well, they got one thing right," she thought to herself. She then remembered her encounter with Marco, but for some reason decided not to reveal this. In her gut she knew he was involved somehow, yet Dr. Perlan would have recognized him if he had been one of his attackers. Unless, that is, he knew his attackers and wasn't telling her.

"No," she lied. "No one noticed me coming back from the dress shop." We can all have our secrets, for now, she thought.

Her bridesmaid's dress! She turned to see it lying carelessly on the floor by the door. She had been going through the motions these past few months pretending to be excited about her sister's wedding. How unimportant it seemed now. She walked over, picked up the crumpled garment bag and tossed it over the back of a chair and absentmindedly smoothed the garment bag with her palms.

"You go and take care of your forehead, doctor. I'll lock the door, put a sign out, and cancel as many of our afternoon appointments as I can reach. We've got a lot of cleaning up to do." Rose knew she needed time to just be with her thoughts and process what had just happened. She allowed her shoulders to slump, caving in around her heavy heart.

CHAPTER TWO: MOUSE GUN

Walking back to her desk, Rose sighed, shaking off the heaviness, and opened the appointment book. She eased a bit as she looked over their light afternoon schedule but couldn't ignore the tension that lingered in the pit of her stomach—a good amount of adrenaline still animating her. As she settled into the phone calls and her thoughts Rose recognized that she felt a sense of excitement and purpose that she had never experienced before. She sensed that the trajectory of her life had changed.

Rose was just finishing up her calls and wondering where to begin cleaning up the mess in the office when she heard the creak of the bathroom door opening.

"Miss Richland…uh…we have another problem."

"Yes Dr. Perlan?" she said, as she thought 'what could it be now?'

"I don't know where my clothes might be. I seem to remember those hoodlums taking them with them, but it's a bit cloudy. Would you mind looking for them?"

Rose sighed as she rose from her chair. What was she

getting herself into? As she searched the waiting room and the treatment room, she began to tidy up—an overturned stool here, a stack of *Life* magazines strewn over there. She even looked for the clothing through the window into the back alley, which was now littered with trash from the overturned metal garbage cans. No white coat or trousers. Even his black Oxfords were missing.

"Now, if I were a bad guy, where would I put an old doctor's clothes?" She realized she was mumbling to herself and hoped that Dr. Perlan couldn't hear her. She did her best problem-solving out loud. Her grandmother told her it was one of her endearing quirks. "I know for certain they didn't take them for their own personal wardrobe." Dr. Perlan's clothes were so shabby that they looked as though they had been eaten by cows and had traveled through their bowels. Rose shook her head and shrugged as she ended her search.

"I think you're right. They did take your clothes." Rose scanned the treatment room one last time and then grabbed the nearest clean medical exam gown.

"For now, I'll give you a gown and perhaps you could wear your coat over it? Until we figure out what to do, that is. But with no shoes you can't walk around here with all this broken glass on the floor." And with no pants, Rose thought to herself, he can't very well walk down Main Street.

She crossed the room to Dr. Perlan's private closet and winced, catching the scent of Old Spice cologne as she searched for his trench coat. The coat slid lopsidedly from the hanger and Rose snatched it in midair. Something cold and metallic pressed against her fingers through the thin fabric. Her heart pounded in her chest as she reached into the pocket. Cold. So very cold. Lifting it into the light, Rose gazed at the tiny silver and black object, no bigger than her hand. More secrets.

A gun.

But not just any gun. Dr. Perlan's gun.

SHIMMER
BY JEREMY CORN

Have you ever had one of those days when you woke up
in a noir? When you woke up to see a tattooed hunter
stalking his prey? The shadows long, dense, and weird –
the light harsh-white like searchlights, and do you
remember the tattooed man, same as me? He stalked
straight through the light and the dark alike, dressed
all in black with his black parson's hat, singing a
psalm, his steady tenor eerie in the stillness. His
quarry–the widow–still alluring despite her grief,
was not afraid, though she ought to be. She let him
catch up to her, and when he did she turned her eyes
up to his–he was so tall–and listened as he said
in that steady tenor, "No more shillyshallying around

now, you hear? Spawn of the Devil's own strumpet—
you're my shame, my crown of thorns." As he raised his
knife to slash through her throat the light shimmered
along the blade, and the widow averted her eyes.

Robin shook me awake then to tell me it was National
Rare Disease Day, which seemed appropriate. I sat up
in bed and watched the dust motes play in the light
while I waited for my cobwebs to clear thinking, even
though they abide and endure, it's an awful hard world
for the littler things. Later that morning, a peculiar
sense of how to be percolating inside my head, we walked
down into the French Quarter looking for coffee, and a
shimmering drag queen—dressed all in sequins, feathers,
and white—passed by us in an alleyway complaining she
was late for church. I don't believe in God per se, but
she looked just like an angel, so we followed, and the
air shimmered around her like radiation or heat haze.
She left a trail behind her of sequins and glitter that
twinkled like diamonds laid in amongst the cobblestones.
The morning sun—playing in those diamonds—spotted my
vision, and I heard the angel in drag saying she was
awakened that very morning by the peals of church bells.

THE CROOKED EYE OF HORUS

BY SUSAN IANNUZZI

1 The Empty Vault

By the time I reached the museum, the rain had soaked through my coat and onto my bad knee. The guard at the side entrance avoided my eyes. People do that when they're standing too close to a mess and hoping it doesn't remember their name.

The vault was two floors down, wrapped in the confidence of concrete. When they opened it, the lights hesitated and then hummed a half-beat late, like they were thinking it over.

I knelt by the pedestal where the Eye of Horus was supposed to be and ran a finger along the stone. Clean cut. No scrape marks.

"This wasn't stolen," I said.

27

"Of course it was," he laughed.

"No," I said. "It *left*."

I rubbed my finger against my thumb. Red-brown dust clung to my skin. Iron, maybe, mixed with something sweeter. Burned resin. The smell pulled a memory loose before I could stop it: my mother, late nights in the conservation lab, gloves ruined, hair carrying that same sharp sweetness home. She used to say old things left marks if you didn't treat them gently.

But never mind *gently*; this one hadn't been treated at all.

The trustee cleared his throat behind me, the sound echoing.

"Security logs show nothing," he said. "No alarms. No badge misuse. No—"

"—mistakes," I finished for him. I stood, my knee arguing the whole way. "I've heard."

He smiled the way men do when they're hoping competence will outrun consequence. His cufflinks caught the light, silver and unburdened. Silver never stays where it's put. That's why some people like it.

I looked past him, at the glass case opposite the pedestal. My reflection stood there patiently, hat brim low, coat darker at the shoulders. When I shifted my weight, it followed—almost. A breath behind. Long enough to make my stomach tighten.

I leaned closer to the glass.

The woman looking back had deeper lines at the mouth. Not worse. Heavier. Like she'd already heard the end of the story I was still pretending was at the beginning.

I straightened. The image caught up.

"Rhea Caulder," I said as I held his gaze. "Who accessed the vault today?" I asked.

The trustee hesitated and then extended his hand. "Jasper Beltran," he said. The lights hummed again, answering something no one had asked out loud.

"Only authorized personnel, Ms. Caulder," he said. "Curators. Conservators."

My thumb still smelled like resin. I wiped it on my coat and didn't feel better.

"Names, Mr. Beltran," I said. "I'll need them in order. Last touch counts."

He nodded, already reaching for his phone. People always believe the last touch matters. They don't like thinking about what waits.

As we left the vault, the temperature changed. Warmer in the hallway, but the air felt thinner somehow, like it had been

borrowed and not properly returned. I caught my reflection
again in the brushed metal of the elevator doors. This time it
didn't lag.

It just watched.

When the doors slid open, the guard from the side entrance
stood there, hands folded, eyes fixed somewhere over my
shoulder. He smelled faintly of copper and wet wool.

"You okay?" I asked him.

He flinched. "Yes, ma'am."

People lie best when the question doesn't sound like an
accusation.

Outside, the rain had eased into a fine mist, the city lights
smearing themselves across the pavement in gold and rust. I
stepped out onto the steps and felt it then, subtle, but certain.
The sense you get when something has been moved that doesn't
like being carried.

Behind me, deep in the museum's concrete belly, something
settled.

And somewhere ahead of me, something waited to be
weighed.

2 The Alley Receipt

Detective Ionescu called just after midnight. She didn't
waste words.

"You still working for the museum?" she asked.

"Yes."

"Then I need you to look at something before it gets
explained away."

"Where?"

A pause. Rain on the line.

"An alley off Mercer," she said. "Come alone. And
Caulder… this isn't off the books. It's just… early."

The alley was three blocks east and a lifetime away.

Police lights lit the brick, alternating in red and blue, and turning the rain into a nervous tic. A uniform stepped aside when he saw me, not because I outranked him, but because everyone recognizes a private detective the way you recognize bad news. You just make room.

The body lay near the dumpster. It resembled a question mark, although no one had asked a question yet. Male. Thirties.

Museum badge clipped to his belt, twisted so the name faced the wall. Someone had tried to be tidy. It showed.

I crouched again, my knee filing a complaint.

"Any other ID?" I asked.

"Wallet's there," the cop said. "Nothing missing."

That was the first wrong thing.

The second was the thread.

Black, waxed, looped once through the eyelids and tied off with a knot you don't learn from sewing kits. The eyes beneath were closed too carefully. Not mercy. Procedure.

"Who found him?" I asked.

"Night cleaner," the cop said. "Says he slipped. Hit his head."

I looked at the wall. No blood spray. No scuff. No story.

The rain had thinned to a mist. Near the body, chalk lines bled into the wet pavement, self-conscious symbols half-erased by weather, stubborn in places where the concrete was cracked. Circles not quite closed. A line crossing another and stopping short.

Incomplete.

I leaned closer. Something smelled faintly sweet. Resin again, cut with something cheaper. Someone had rushed the materials, not the act.

The dead man's hand was clenched around a scrap of paper. I eased it free.

Names. Six of them. Written carefully, as if care still mattered at the end.

Mine wasn't there.

Yet.

I stood and caught my reflection in the chrome of the dumpster lid. It looked straight back at me, steady as a verdict.

Behind me, Mara Ionescu shifted her weight, her coat hanging off her shoulders like it had given up the argument years ago. She never bought clothes that wanted anything from her.

"You know him?" she asked.

"I know his job," I said.

"What was it?"

I folded the paper and slid it into my pocket. The rain ticked softly against metal.

"Touching things that didn't belong to him," I said.

Mara's mouth tightened.

"You think this is some kind of message?" she asked, motioning towards the chalk.

I looked at the symbols again, at what hadn't quite been finished.

"No," I said. "I think it's proof someone's already been paid."

Thunder rolled somewhere upriver.

I stepped back into the street, gold light stretching across the wet asphalt, and felt it again, that shift, like weight being adjusted when no one's looking.

Someone had paid.

Someone else hadn't.

And whatever balance this was meant to settle, it wasn't done with me yet.

THERE'S NO SPYING IN BASEBALL!

BY JOHN AL

At first, it had been the ritual's agony that haunted her. But looking back on it all after more than fifty annual payouts for "trusting her intuition," she could no longer recall a Designated face from more than five years ago, much less the Discards. And that included the Discards from the early days that had a habit of visiting her while she slept, some for decades at a stint. The agony had run its course.

How upsetting.

Back when the yearly Designation took place at Forbes Field, the agony arose from tangling with the morality of it. World War II suffocated that insistent virtue right out of her. Uncle Sam surrendered more sons and husbands to friendly fire in one day than she discarded in a decade. Then after Forbes came the first year at the new stadium. Well, that was an Opening Day unlike any other. Not from her annual morbid Designation though. That didn't change, and according to Langley, it never would. By the time 1970 rolled around, she became swallowed up in the logistics of how some benign yet vulgar ritual, undetectable for decades now, could just up and move to the other side of town without the most curious and well-funded eyes of the CIA's enemies finding out about it. But that riddle, too, lost its sheen by '72. Of course, it didn't hurt that the Pittsburgh Pirates were defending World Series Champions, and she'd even managed to bump into Roberto Clemente himself that game. Thankfully, it didn't happen in the umpire's locker room during the 7th-inning stretch. That would've been serendipitously tragic. She would've designated Clemente regardless, no matter who the other Discard might've been.

Today, though. Today was different. Clemente had been fish food for over a quarter century, the phrase 'World Series Champion' was practically contraband to the new ownership, and her granddaughter Katie had just turned 14. She wasn't quite old enough yet, not even close really, but it wasn't her that Father Time had cornered into this transition of power.

Katie's mother had agreed to drop her off near the Gate D Pylon, since the arrangement had historically included exactly two tickets to Opening Day. Grandma straightened her Coke vendor name tag, tied her black and gold bandanas to her belt, adjusted her Coca-Cola hat (it was the fifteen-year anniversary of the Mean Joe Greene commercial!), checked to make sure the needle was sheathed and opened her arms as wide as they would go for her only grandchild.

The journey to their seats had been an assault on the senses. Pigeons balanced themselves on the wires supporting the safety nets. The sounds of gold-digging vendors, but who was she to judge? They wore their uniforms for survival, she wore hers for subterfuge. The scent of over-grilled hotdogs. The taste—or lack thereof—of her annual Iron City beer. (Katie opted for a sundae in a mini-helmet. She refused the first one because they tried to serve it to her in a Cubs cap. Good kid. Good instincts. She was going to need them.) They arrived at their section right behind home plate just as Katie asked for some napkins to finish the job that licking her fingers could not quite accomplish.

Every year that the woman had been doing this, she had gone to the games alone, despite receiving her customary two tickets at Will Call, per the arrangement with Langley. Every year she tried enjoying the game before the inevitable 7th-inning stretch. Every year she failed. It was one of the few emotional journeys that had not come and gone since the first time she "trusted her intuition." Every year she was consumed with equal parts anxiety and guilt, understandably so. This year, however, would be garnished with an appetizer even more foul tasting

than the flat Iron. Really, though, what was the point of easing
Katie into her new assignment with some gradual sugar-coated
chat that crescendos into a capital crime tutorial? Katie had no
choice in the matter, same as it had been for her grandmother.
And once she maneuvered the ethics of it, then she could
anticipate another 20 or 30 years of debating whether the
arbitrary decision model or the act itself weighed more heavily.
She wasn't deconstructing and digesting all of that in six and a
half innings; the kid was currently losing her battle to keep hot
fudge off her chamois.

The two candidates were told to expect someone matching
the description of Katie's grandmother. They were instructed
every year to expect her during the 7th-inning stretch in the
umpire's locker room. Sometimes they were sitting, sometimes
they were standing, sometimes one of each. In the late 60s the
woman would discard whichever one was sitting, as if that was
some kind of honor worthy system. In the 70s, she mostly went

by manners. First one to behave rudely became the Discard. Tone can be the difference between life and death.

It wasn't until the 80s that she experienced two major breakthroughs. The first was changing the weapon. (Silenced Berettas had been her preference, but then the frisky ushers stationed at all the entrances had put an end to that.) The second was just ordering the Designate to eliminate the Discard, keeping her hands clean. That only lasted a few years, mostly on account of the rather delicate hostage situation she instigated in '89. In fact, that likely expedited the sobering reflection that resulted in deputizing her granddaughter today, a few years earlier than she would have liked.

Katie's eyes were as wide as they were submissive, like when she heard Mr. Rogers' voice for the first time. Her entire childhood, as abbreviated as it was about to become, had been spent fearing the velvet ropes and Do Not Enter signs that governed her choices and exploration. And here Grandma bypassed a gauntlet of them with nothing more than a confident stride and a lazy disguise. Katie clutched her souvenir mini-helmet with one hand and latched onto Grandma's Coca-Cola vest with the other. She hadn't done that since the two of them watched *Night of the Living Dead* at the Evans City Drive-In on Halloween weekend. Good instincts. Good kid.

The woman took one last look around the umpire's locker room. Same smell of fresh bats and Bengay. Same crooked plaque. Nothing but a sterile examination room to her that she couldn't wait to forget. For her granddaughter? An emotional Rubicon and cork-scented prison, forever calcified.

"Good evening, gentlemen." She pulled Katie a little closer. "Before we begin, I want you both to meet Katie. She's my granddaughter. And she's my replacement. Honey, you stay right there and listen real good."

The woman sat down at the trainer's table, across from the

two men. "Go ahead, Moustache."

"The combination is 34 left, 27 right, 8 left."

No change. Again. Never did learn what exactly they think those numbers unlock.

"And what about you, Sideburns?" She pointed at the other one.

"Suitcase weighed just over 20 lbs before the handoff."

Sounds like a million bucks in hundreds. Again. That was the conclusion she came to every year regarding that allegedly priceless scrap of intel. She wondered what fib Katie would tell herself?

How upsetting.

"OK fellas. You can both relax. Congratulations, you made it! Welcome to the CIA. There's only one more thing we need to take care of, and then you can start sipping martinis and slapping chesty women." She stood and returned to Katie's side. "For security purposes before we move on, I need to blindfold both of you. Then I'm going to check you for listening devices and make sure you're not smuggling anything, and then you'll be on your way to the final rendezvous."

The woman pulled Katie's black and gold bandana off of her head while removing her own from her belt, tossing them both on the table. The men obliged.

"Mouths wide open please," she blurted once they were done blinding themselves. "Now say ahhh!"

She looked down at Katie, pressed one finger to her lips, slowly nodded her head and pointed to her ears. Then she walked right up to Sideburns, pulled out the syringe she'd been bringing to Opening Day since they installed metal detectors and plunged her little Sword of Damocles underneath his tongue. She observed the shock of his body's disbelief while the nerve agent trumped any follow-up commands. His body went limp so suddenly that Grandma struggled to keep him upright in his seat, her arthritic grip far from useful. Father Time couldn't help himself, even after she conceded to an argument he had never lost and never would.

The woman blurted something unintelligible while trying to control the potato sack of a corpse, causing Moustache to reach for his blindfold for a peek.

"Grandma!" Katie spouted while pointing. Good kid. Good instincts.

Just as Grandma created distance between herself and moustache, the man sprung out of his seat, his uncovered eyes scanning his surroundings, ostensibly for a weapon.

"Let's all take a breath there, peek-a-boo. Nobody else needs to get hurt." Grandma glanced at her Katie. She was frozen, her face aghast. The woman recognized that look of emotional annihilation. Apparently, it's hereditary. "Listen, it's over. I already told you to relax, didn't I? Mission's complete. You've been Designated for the Agency. He was Discarded. Doesn't need to escalate beyond that."

The man was now hyperventilating.

"Who the hell are you?" he managed to squeeze out between breaths.

"Told you already, Moustache. I'm Katie's grandmother." The woman slowly returned the syringe to her pocket, the man's eyes straying from the needle only once to check the fresh corpse for any signs of life. "He was a finalist, same as you. CIA only needs one, and they prefer the better of the two. They leave it to me to decide which one's the keeper. All the training and high scores in the world can't hold a candle to women's intuition. At least according to Langley. Congratulations on your Designation."

Grandma pulled the bandana off the Discard while extending her hand toward the other, beckoning the Designate to return the bandana he was clutching.

"Now, I'm sure you have an awful lot of questions. The Designates always do. Bad news is I'm not going to answer a single one. One, because that ain't my job, and two, we don't have time. Good news is that you'll be able to ask all the questions you want once you're safely out of the stadium." The woman swiped the bandana from his trembling hand and extended her other hand toward the umpire's exit. "You head through that door now and you're going to see a man wearing a Pirates cap and holding an umbrella. He's your new North Star. Now if you'll excuse us, my Katie and I have a very uncomfortable conversation to get through before her mother picks her up 15 outs from now. Twelve if we don't manage to give up the tying run."

The crowd, oblivious to the changing of the guard in the umpire's locker room, serenaded the grounds crew tidying up the field. "Strike one, two, three, you're out at the old ballgame!"

Right on time. Again. The cleanup crew, Moustache, and his handler would have another routine Opening Day. No delays and no surprises. Again.

Katie, on the other hand, still didn't look so good. Watching your own grandmother cram a corpse into a shipping container meant for baseball bats likely had something to do with it. The woman made it appear as effortless as possible all while flippantly reciting the uncomfortable conversation she'd been dreading since Father Time made his opening arguments in 1989.

It was so much easier than she thought it would be.

How upsetting.

Was her detachment a professional courtesy, or were Grandma's instincts that had been on the CIA payroll for over half a century making sure Father Time didn't go anywhere near her precious little granddaughter?

It was so rejuvenating to lament the answer and finally feel something a little different on Opening Day.

"Don't worry Katie, we'll just tell Mom you ate a little too much ice cream. Now let me show you how this syringe works before we go back to our seats."

Good kid. Good instincts.

FINLEY'S PLEASURE BAR
BY MEGHAN SNATCHKO

In the quickening January light, the asphalt of the parking lot behind Hinkley Analytical Lab appears as a black hole. The rising sun turns the sky blood red. Kara always hears one of her grandmother's favorite sayings on mornings like this.

Red sky in the morning, Sailors' warning…

She looks at her wrist. 8:03 AM.

Kara, it's over.

"Betrayal like this tastes like pennies."

A violent exhalation escapes her lips and peppers the cold glass with tiny spit bubbles. She turns from the square window and faces him. "Oh really? How would you know?"

Detective Forrester is crouched on the floor but pivots on his toes to look up at her. "I'm not dumb and I've been four years old before. How do you not know what pennies taste like?"

Kara puts her hands on her hips. "You know that's not what I meant by that question. Really, Brad? So, it's going to be like that now, is it?"

"Huh? Like what? You know, this week is extremely hectic for me. I really don't need you adding to it. Never mind, let's just get back to examining the scene."

She watches his steel gaze soften as he turns his attention back to the dead woman on the floor. She plunges her hand into the left pocket of her trench coat. Her watch gets caught on the fabric. Every fiber of her being curses her twin sister's idea for a New Year's Resolution. *God Dammit, Kimmy.* She should be exhaling strawberry clouds of nicotine right now, but it comes out as "FUUUUUUUUCK" instead.

He tenses at the expletive. Then he sucks his teeth.

Who does this guy think he is? He should be the last to judge.

Kara notices a flashing light on the lab printer. Its rhythm lulls her into a memory of the last time they were in bed together. She thinks about all the sweat that soaked her sheets. *How much am I going to save on laundry detergent?* "Heh. That's great."

He snaps his head toward her. "What's great? What did you find?"

Kara points at the printer with a gloved finger. "Oh, um. I think we have a clue. The printer is displaying a message: 'Printing paused. 3 of 5 pages complete. Clear jam in Tray 1.' And look, the output is empty. If we clear the jam, I bet the rest of the pages will come out. Maybe pages that the killer didn't want us to see. We need to get it dusted before we can check."

Kara puts a pink post-it on the printer to let the tech know it's a priority and continues to examine the disarray.

Why am I never the priority?

A few years ago, when she was first promoted to Homicide Detective, she was 31 and laughably green. Her new partner was almost ten years older, but he never talked down to her.

"Hey, the way you handled yourself with that crazy lady back there. I have to say, I've seen officers twice your age and size back down to some hippy with a hammer. I thought she was going to start swinging and so I backed up. You didn't. I think once the filthy pig saw she couldn't scare you, she realized she had to let us in her son's apartment. I couldn't believe it. Great job!"

Before she could thank him, he squeezed her shoulder and looked into her eyes, tilting his head down to demand her gaze.

"No, really. I'm impressed. Hey, do you mind if I call you Kara?"

"I suppose…if I can call you Brad."

"Deal."

***

Late last year, after they had successfully wrangled a confession out of a man who had strangled his ex-girlfriend to death, they found themselves on two bar stools in a smoky dive called Finley's Pleasure Bar. A cop bar barely on the outskirts of the city was the perfect place to celebrate. The drinks flowed.

The room got fuzzy.

Like putting on a plush robe straight out of the dryer.

Brad put down his I.C. Light and grabbed a handful of peanuts from the bowl on the bar. "Wanna hear a really inappropriate joke?"

She sipped her Bacardi and Diet. "Always."

"Okay, why didn't Superman stop the planes from hitting the towers on 9/11?" He popped a peanut in his mouth.

Kara looked past the twinkling string lights that lined the bar. "Hmmmm, I give up. Why?" She took a sip of her drink.

"Because he was in a wheelchair!"

Kara had never done an actual spit-take but proceeded to

spew sticky liquid all over the wooden bar top. She wiped her mouth with a cocktail napkin. "Oh, that is bad."

"Too soon?"

"Maybe. Tell me another."

That night, Brad made her laugh so hard she almost peed her pants. As the edges of the wood-paneled room dulled, she listened to his jokes and found herself inching closer. She talked about her parents' divorce, and he opened up about his marriage.

"Linds and I got together when we were basically teenagers. Fuck, we've been together over 20 years! We aren't the same people we were back then, you know? When I come home after a long day… I want to relax and have a nice meal with easy conversation. Instead, she completely ignores me or nags me about bullshit until bedtime. I swear, it's like I only exist for my paycheck or to take out the trash. I don't know which is worse."

Kara didn't speak. She was lost in the way his jaw flexed as he spoke. The vein at his temple pulsed faster as he looked straight ahead toward the glittering bottles along the mirrored wall. He was studying her reflection. She startled when he turned quickly and locked her eyes to his.

"It's nice to talk to somebody who actually knows how hard this job can be. The shit we deal with... it's dark. My problem is trying to get the dead-eyed stare of a seven-year-old victim out of my mind so I can sleep. Meanwhile, she's devastated because Starbucks ran out of coconut milk last week. She's ridiculous. You get it, though. We don't even have to talk. You just get me."

She leaned toward him and fell off her barstool.

He caught her and placed her back on the seat. "Alright, no way you're driving home. I think the bartender got a little heavy-handed with the rum. I'll take you home and pick you up to get your car in the morning. Finish your drink and we'll go."

The ride to her townhome was silent. When they arrived,

he got out when she did.

"Brad, I'm fine. You don't have to escort me to my door. I'm okay now."

"I know, but I'd feel a lot better if I made sure you got in safely."

Kara decided to let him and started walking up the steps.

Brad stopped on the second step from the top. She turned to face him. For once, they were eye-to-eye. "Thanks for driving me home. I had fun tonight."

Brad took two steps up and looked down at her. He squeezed her shoulder. "I had fun too." Then he turned and started walking toward his car. "Have a good night, Kara."

She couldn't stop herself. "Yeah. So, I know it's late, but, um, do you want to come up for some coffee or something?"

He stopped in his tracks and addressed the dark, "More than anything."

"You told her you joined a pool league? I get it. Sticks, balls, pockets. Not too far from the truth." Kara kissed his fingertips.

He winked playfully at her. "Nice rack." Brad got out of bed and after a bit of searching, found his pants draped over the lampshade. "I could have told her I was here in your bed. She doesn't care what I do, just as long as I'm not bothering her and the credit card bill keeps getting paid. But yes, I told her I joined a pool league that has matches every Thursday night. You're welcome."

She smacked his butt. "No, you're welcome!"

He turned and grabbed her ankles. "Thank you. I'm gonna show you how much I appreciate that you are not my wife."

As he pulled her to his side of her bed, she yelled out, "I really appreciate it, too!"

The fluorescent glare on the overturned water bottle in the corner of the break room snaps her back to 2024. Near the refrigerator, a mineralized puddle mixes with sticky red. It forms a watercolor swirl of pink on the linoleum that looks like it came from the end of a paintbrush, not a massive head wound.

He really thinks he's a good person. BRAAAAAAAD. Sounds like a sound made by a fainting goat. Or worse, a dumb woman in the throes of passion on a weekend getaway to Cleveland. Stroll Inn and Fall Deep.

"Detective Burke! Are you listening to me? I asked what time Ms. Jensen normally left the office on Thursdays?"

I am not her secretary. How in the fuck would I know the schedule of a random scientist in a forensics lab? "It's **Doctor** Jensen and I'll check with her supervisor… or maybe we can see her schedule on her phone. Is there one in her pocket?"

"I didn't see one."

"That's weird. Perhaps the killer took it."

"Good insight. Make a note to check with the family to see if she even owned one."

The demand barely masquerading as praise makes her stomach flip. "After a year of… whatever we were… why now?"

"She got close to finding out about us and I can't risk it."

Kara held her breath.

He sighed. "I have to stay with her. We have a family together. A house. I can't just throw that all away. Also, have you considered what would happen if this got out? Both of our reputations would be ruined. We need to be practical and stay calm. You're not gonna make this hard for me, are you? Trust me, you don't want to do that."

He turns and crouches down, tenderly moving a lock of hair from the face of the dead woman. The gesture screams familiarity.

"Detective Forrester, did you know the victim?"

"Of course I didn't. Are you crazy?" He stands and writes something in a fresh notepad. "But, I can tell you that Amelia probably did know who did this to her. There are no defensive wounds on her hands or arms and the only blow as far as I can tell was directly to her face with something hard and sharp. She wasn't expecting it. That's why I said it was betrayal. I have some ideas, but I'm curious if you have any guesses on the murder weapon?"

She barely hears him as limerence swirls with shame and pushes all helpful thoughts from her grasp. *"Did you actually have a dead bedroom or is that another lie?"*

Did I say that out loud?

He says nothing as an icy gust rattles the square window.

This bastard has been double dipping with his wife the whole time.

A sound coming from his pocket pauses her expanding wrath.

BTHHHHP. BTHHHHP. BTHHHHP.

Kara stares directly into Brad's eyes, eroding the stone mask he'd been wearing since this morning. He blinks, she doesn't.

"You asked about the murder weapon? If I had to guess, I'd say it's something extremely sharp, exceptionally smooth, and easily concealed. I have two questions though: Where did you go after you left my place last night? And why is your pocket vibrating when your phone is right over there on top of your coat?"

His mouth opens and shuts, but nothing comes out.

He looks a lot like a dying fish.

Clarity.

I don't care about what lie he is struggling to make up.

His business was no longer any of hers.

Precocious

Flight.

THE WRITING ON THE WALL

BY BEVERLEE BLAIR

i.

Sam was the gargoyle. He looked out on the town from his perch on the ramparts. He could see the cornerstone of the building where the forgotten spoke in riddles in pencil and crayon and chalk and marker. He had passed this rare, derelict building many times over the months since school began because his driver, a young woman and former police cadet, varied their route from home to his school. She'd seemed giddily obsessed with this route. A vacant apartment in a building in a not yet gentrified neighborhood had drawn her to it. She'd visited the apartment and spoke about it often as he sat in his booster seat behind her, his strawberry, blond hair covered by a brownish wig, covered by a baseball cap. She was right. It was a beautiful, old building, and he smiled when she told him about the large rooms and high ceilings and lots of light, but it was the other one, nearby, that interested him. The one where people wrote things.

It had taken two passes before he could decipher one line written there: *Our country is not his 'ho*. His friend, Nemo, tried to explain but gave up when Sam continued to stare blankly back at him.

It was on the fourth or fifth pass that Sam had seen something that should not have been there.

ii.

Nemo disembarked from the van that brought him and three or four others to school. He felt the others breeze by him, shouting 'hello' to no one in particular or to someone they knew or because they'd been told again and again that they must look people in the eye and say that word. He climbed the steps, stood beside Mrs. Guthrie, the only teacher always – apparently – glad to see him. He turned and waited.

He tried to take in his surroundings as others did naturally, but any connection to sky, temperature, activity or mood, eluded him. He could see that the sky was blue, that the trees had begun to leaf and to bloom, that other students emerged from vehicles that had slowed and stopped in front of the complex of modest brick buildings that made up this school, but none of that touched him. Nothing would until first Beth, then Sam arrived. Before them, nothing and no one had since his sister died.

At last, they came. Beth wrenched open the car door, came out and slammed the door behind her. She didn't say "goodbye" or even wave to her grandfather, who didn't look at her at all. He couldn't wait to get away. They had done the best they could.

Sam arrived. His driver, a young woman with military bearing, opened the door for him. He climbed down from his booster seat and got out. She closed the door.

"Have a good day, Sam."

He climbed the steps without acknowledging Beth. Nemo knew that something was very wrong. Sam had come, but nothing of him was present. Beth turned as Sam passed her. She looked up at Nemo, stunned and worried. It would not be a good day for her, but it was not Sam's fault and she knew that. Nemo and Beth watched as Sam continued up the steps and opened the door into their school. Once inside, he did not remove his cap and his wig as had been his custom.

It was not going to be a good day for Sam. Nemo put his hand on Beth's shoulder. She shrugged it off and went up the steps to the door. She did not say "hey" in answer to Geordie's "Hey, Beth." She did not notice that he winced at her failure.

It was not going to be a good day for either Beth or Sam. Or for Geordie, for that matter.

iii.

He was the gargoyle, looking out over the roofs of buildings that meant nothing to him, were nothing to him. He gazed out to the place with the writing. He was afraid for the first time in a long time.

He'd kept outside voices from reaching his ears for longer
this time, but one broke through his defenses. Torn from his
aerie, he fell backward, landing with a thud and, looking around
him, unseeing, he blinked the ramparts from his eyes.

"Sammy," not loud, but firm. Little more than a whisper,
really.

"Sam," he replied, re-focusing. Only his father called him
"Sammy," cooing, terrible.

iv.

Beth did not groan out loud when the arithmetic lesson was
scrawled on the chalkboard and accompanying work sheets were
passed down each aisle of desks front to back. They were the
same math problems as yesterday and the day before. Nemo had
told her that Marlie needed to hear things over and over again
so that she could learn. Repetition was Marlie's salvation. Marlie
in her turn served as an impediment to Beth's frustrations
exploding, painting the walls obscenely.

If it hadn't been for Nemo, Beth might never have known
tenderness for someone at the center of a storm. He lived there,
too. And so did she.

She didn't notice at first that in doing the sums yet again,
her pencil had torn through the worksheet, shredding it with
every correct answer. Marlie, not having noticed, was grinning at
her from across the classroom, waiting for her turn to work one
on one with the teacher. Beth smiled back. She held on.

Be calm.

Innocent, both teacher and teaching assistant, kneeling,
gave their full attention to each of the eight other students in the
classroom, inquiring and answering voices low, patience met
with confusion, patience met with understanding, patience met
with glee, patience met with tears. Geordie, waiting his turn
could not snap out of growing anxiety at Beth's not having

smiled in answer to his greeting this morning. His anxiety morphed slowly into anger.

Something struck Beth on the side of her head. She looked down. An eraser. Looked up. Geordie leered, blocked Marlie out.

"Crazy bitch," he mouthed and motioned, the index finger whirling at the side of his head, the universal sign.

"Ooh, Geordie," Marlie intoned, barely above a whisper, accusing, warning, wagging her own finger at the offender, her eyes widening.

The teaching assistant glanced up, having missed the instigation, but she turned immediately back to the task already in hand and would miss any retaliation.

Why had Geordie done that?

Be calm.

I'm trying.

Beth felt betrayed again by someone she'd thought was her friend.

Breathe.

I am breathing.

Twice in one day. Betrayed. First Sam…

Was that it? Had she, too, failed to do something that had been expected of her? What?

Give him hell.

She wanted to sign something, but she had not yet learned any swear words.

Beth stood up, her sums crumbled and torn in one hand, her pencil snapped in the other. Geordie's ears reddened. Inner turmoil distorted her face, her hands, her back, turned her into the alien she knew herself to be.

"Geordie. Beth. Sit down, please," crooned their teacher, soothing, hopeful, too late.

Give 'em hell.

Geordie sat down, but Beth could not. Her breath came from her in heaving waves. She was removed from her classroom and as she passed the room where Sam was learning to sign...

Something in the air came prickly over Sam's skin, seeped through renewed defenses. He looked up in time to see Beth still heaving.

"No. No. No..." not signing.

Sam had to be removed from the room before the others in his class could be caught up in his loss of control. His teacher understood that she, alone, must supervise his exit. She collected Sam herself, gently, unhurried. He seemed to come willingly. Her teaching assistant's stern demeanor was less an impediment than a dare to remaining students. Once the door closed on Sam and his teacher, they grew restless.

When Nemo saw the bizarre parade that was Beth then Sam passing by his classroom door, he leaped from his chair, his eyes, beseeching. Mrs. Guthrie did not hesitate.

"Miss Rogers, please accompany Nemo to the director's office."

They'd had a bad day, spreading contagion between them beginning with Sam's disappearance into himself and carrying on to Beth's natural ferocity pulling her apart – 'be calm' in one direction, 'let 'er rip' in the other – through to Nemo's determined guardianship.

v.

It turned out that it had been a bad day for many. When they arrived in the lobby of the administration building, four other students were already there, their shoes kicking the legs of their chairs in a rhythmless percussion. Miss Crowe, presiding over the lobby, maintained order by some unknown but unimpeachable quirk of personality. At a look, they were still, but it didn't take long before they were at it again.

Nemo, Sam, and Beth were brought to her desk and, at a

single nod, two things happened: their teacher and teaching assistants left the room, and the three sat down in chairs nearest them, Nemo and Beth cocooning Sam, whose eyes were fixed on the floor. Miss Crowe picked up a glass from her desk, took a sip, surveyed her realm, set the glass down again. If she swallowed, no one knew it.

Her phone rang. She answered, "Yes?" and a rare frown creased her forehead. "I understand."

She stood up from her desk. One, sweeping look from her pinned the students to their seats. She went to the door of the school's director, knocked briskly twice and entered.

Earnest murmuring emitted through the door. The students, marooned in their seats, could not have heard the words that nevertheless hovered over them.

Miss Crowe came out, gathered the four students who had preceded the three and left the lobby with them.

"She should have been a teacher," Nemo whispered before the door closed behind them. He sensed Miss Crowe's answering smile.

Silence sang around them.

Nemo reached out, took the hands of his fellow sojourners, squeezed gently, let go, sat back in his seat.

Miss Crowe returned, glancing idly at the three. Sitting once more behind her desk, she sipped delicately from her glass and locked her gaze upon the door, which opened as if on her command. She considered standing, thought better of it, sipped instead.

Mrs. Guthrie entered first, followed by a man wearing a dark, grey suit. He swiped the jacket aside so that Miss Crowe could not miss the gold badge fixed to the right of his belt buckle. Nemo saw it, too, along with a hint of the man's shoulder holster. Nemo stiffened. If the officer noticed, he did not react, glancing instead at Sam. Both missed Beth's reaction to him: *be calm* reached out to him, beckoning; *give them hell* froze her solid where she sat.

"She's expecting you." Miss Crowe nodded and this new pair entered the office of the director.

Miss Crowe's phone rang again.

"Yes?... Of course…". She hung up, muttering, "My last nerve."

She stood, wagged a finger at the three, a gesture they well knew.

"Be still and know that I'm still in charge."

She left.

Nemo waited a beat after the door closed behind her, wagged a finger in the direction of the two in perfect Crowe mimicry. Then he went to her desk, drained the water from her glass, shook any remaining droplets from it and placed the open end on the director's door. He put his ear to the base of the glass and his eyes on the door into the lobby, willing Miss Crowe not to return too soon. He heard the people inside talking, his brain filling in what at first seemed garbled:

"The first victim was a black kid named Isaac. He told us that 'some nasty-smelling white guy snatched me.' The perpetrator put a hood over his head, threw him in what sounded like a supermarket cart, threw something over him, and took off. Isaac said the cart thumped and bumped for several blocks so fast that he couldn't stand up. Then he thought he was inside a building somewhere. He heard someone say, 'I got me one!' and there was laughter. Then someone shrieked 'That is not my son. Get him out of here.' He was returned to the area where he'd been taken. There were two more incidents. Both boys, both around seven years old. One blonde. One a redhead. Both were released after someone screamed that it wasn't his son. All three said the perpetrators smelled bad."

"Why are you here?"

"We only have a description of the ringleader because one of those smelly men was found hogtied in a ditch. He gave us a description of the

vi.

Nemo risked everything when he did not immediately move away from that door, but he couldn't. At last, wrenching himself from his stupor, he stage whispered, "It worked!" to Beth, whose hand rested lightly on Sam's stooped back.

Nemo returned the glass to Miss Crowe's desk and sat down, his mind, seething. He knew that the smelly man had said nothing else because he died on the way to the hospital.

vii.

Stealth became his prime directive. He had to do something. He couldn't let anyone hurt Sam. He turned over everything he had heard, and he planned. As his plan took shape, he wrote everything down. It helped him think. When he knew that he could not implement his plan by himself, he began

slipping notes into Beth's hands and Sam's books and pockets.
He could not tell if Sam understood any of it.

viii.

He was the gargoyle on the ramparts looking over the city
to the place where his mother lay broken. He needed badly to
see her. To talk with her. But he wasn't allowed. If he had to be
his father's son, just this once, to help Nemo, then he would. He
must. And he knew that his father, hyper focused on one thing,
would never get the joke.

He had found Nemo's first note in the outside, zipper
pocket of his backpack, where he kept his pencils. It read
Kite #1
We are going to stop Sam's father.

Sam did not know why Nemo called the notes 'kites' but he
numbered them so that Sam knew he had to look elsewhere – a
pants pocket or a book – to find one he may have missed. The
kites, with their slowly evolving plan, were the buoy that saved
him from disappearing altogether. He needed to hang on—to
keep hold of himself—until he could see his mother. His mother
would get the joke, and they would laugh.

ix.

If Nemo had held the open end of a glass to the closed
door of the teachers' lounge the next day, he would have heard
the conversation taking place between the Director, Mrs.
Guthrie, and Detective Donnelly.

"On my way in, I saw children signing. Do you have deaf
students here?"

"No. We teach all of our students American Sign Language.
Studies have shown that it helps with communication, cognition,
and empathy."

"I see."

"Ours is a relatively small student body. Our students are
learning disabled in some way. But learning disabled is a kind of

umbrella that covers a variety of aspects. Sam, Beth and Nemo were among those disabled not by defect or neurological deficits, but by trauma. They seemed to have developed a kind of radar that allowed them to find one another. As if trauma were something they shared but could not have expressed. Sam, the youngest of them, seems to nest in their sometimes prickly, inexplicable bond."

"For the moment, none of that matters."

"I beg to differ." Mrs. Guthrie stopped, considered what she was about to share with this man. Gave in to the impulse. "I was in my thirties when I dreamed I was running away from a man I knew wanted to hurt me. I ran into a crowd, hoping I would lose him, but he hurt some of those people in his effort to get to me. I stopped and turned around. I didn't know where it came from, but there was suddenly a two-by-four in my hands. I let him get close enough for me to beat the living crap out of him. I had to make him stop. When I woke up, I knew I had killed him and I was horrified by the thought.

"I don't know how much you know about Sam's and Nemo's situations. Nemo saw his twin sister gunned down in front of him. She died in his arms. Yes, that scarred him in ways you and I cannot fathom, but know this. He would never, never do anything to hurt Sam or Beth. He would, however, go to hell to protect them.

"Sam's mother is still recovering from injuries suffered at his father's hands. As you know, Sam's father was never caught, and Sam was placed in protective custody with a psychologist and social worker who fostered children in his circumstances. His aunt and uncle had his mother moved to a rehabilitation facility near them. They visited Sam and his mother in tandem until Sam was released into their care. They hired private security and registered Sam with our school. I can tell you nothing about Beth. The unspeakable events of her life were sealed."

"We have patrols looking for Sam's father. Should we be watching the children, too?"

x.

Nemo searched the places where the homeless were known to congregate and to live. He roamed downtown streets until he found a rundown building near the center of the town. It took up an entire block. He circled it, reading what had been scrawled on the foundation stones. He found *"Our country is not his 'ho"* and stopped cold. An old man came out of the shadow of a recessed doorway. Behind him was a shopping cart filled with blankets and cans and plastic bags filled with God knew what.

"What you want?"

"Where is everybody?"

"Cops came. Cleared all us out. Me, I come back. It's safe now. That devil didn't come back."

"But where did the rest of them go?"

"Oh, there's places around town. Parks and such. Or the woods outside of town."

"What about the devil? Where'd he go?"

"One them places. You don't want to know."

And with that, he pushed by Nemo, looked both ways and started to cross the street.

"Don't be messin' with my stuff," he called over his shoulder.

"Wait! Can you help me get inside this way? I won't touch anything. I promise."

He found himself in a courtyard. To his right, another door opened onto a marble floored lobby with a marble staircase. He went up. He walked through an open door into a room overlooking the courtyard. The only direct access to the courtyard from the street were two, chained gates. A tree, long dead, leaned against the wall just below the window where he stood looking out.

66

This was perfect. He managed to extract a promise from the man, then he thanked him and went home.

xi.

The next day, Nemo searched as many parks as he could find. Nothing. He went further afield, scanning the hills outside the town. There was a war memorial park along a sparsely populated and narrow road into those hills. He went up.

He heard muted laughter and shouts and grunts, but it was difficult to see anything among the dense brush and trees along

the hillside. He didn't like it there. It felt as if the woods were full
of monsters. He went home.

xii.

The next morning, he waited on the steps, Mrs. Guthrie,
behind him, his fist in his pocket, closed around the last of his
kites. Beth arrived. She threw open the car door and slammed it
closed behind her. Her grandfather did not wave. He could not
get away fast enough. Beth climbed the steps and turned and
waited.

Sam did not come.

Mrs. Guthrie took Nemo and Beth by the hand and led
them into the school. Instead of dropping them off at their first
classes, she guided them to the office of the director and left
them with Miss Crowe. Miss Crowe smiled at them. Bewildered,
neither took a seat. She ignored this and went to the director's
door, knocked briskly, went inside without closing the door
behind her.

"Show them in."

Miss Crowe nodded them into the presence of the director.

"Please. Sit down."

They sat in chairs facing her desk.

"Sam's uncle phoned the school this morning to tell us that
he would not be returning to school. Sam is terribly upset. His
uncle asked if we could arrange that you, Nemo, and you, Beth,
could be taken to their home to say goodbye. If it's all right with
your guardians, one of the school vans will take you to there
tomorrow after school so that you can say your goodbyes. You've
both been asked to stay for dinner. The van will take you home
afterward. Is that agreeable to you?"

It was.

In passing after their first class, Nemo slipped kite number
19 into Beth's hands. It read *Pack up the stuff I asked you to get, wrap
it like a gift and bring it to school tomorrow.*

Dinner that evening was a somber affair. It was always somber. Not sad. It was heavier than sad. His father read the newspaper. His mother scrolled on her phone. They seemed to cut, to lift their forks to their mouths, to chew as if on automatic. Both, shut down, just going through the motions of work and housework and bridge and book club and two meals shared and sometimes his mother forgot that there should only be three plates and they could hardly bare to look at their son. How much longer would it be that way?

"I'm going for a walk," Nemo announced, quietly.

"Don't forget to take your key," his father said, glancing across the table at his son. His gaze did not linger. Slipped away.

"Don't be long." His mother did not look up.

"I won't."

He went back to the woods. It was still light enough to see where he was going. As if he knew where he was going. He left the trail and began walking up the brush covered hill. Aside from the swishing aside of small branches, he heard nothing, but his skin felt alive, tingling, electric, swarming with something he could not see. His ears rang.

"You're back."

He jumped, slipped backward. Dirt and stones rattled down the hill behind him. He managed to turn around and found a man standing between him and the trail. He was tall and he wore a long, black wool coat, the collar turned up. Nemo could not have mistaken him. His long, curly, strawberry blonde hair was so like Sam's. He oozed a welcoming malevolence, seemed to defy time and space like a shapeshifter Nemo had once seen in a movie. He was a myth. A non-being. He spoke to Nemo in a lilting, crooning sort of way.

"What are you doing here all by yourself? I've seen you here before, though, haven't I? Do you mean to join us? Have you brought us anything to liven our evening in the woods?"

Nemo focused on the bridge of the man's nose. He did not want to look into his eyes. And he did not want to answer any of the questions being posed to him. To enter into conversation with Sam's dad would somehow close a door behind him. And lock it.

"I know the one you're looking for," Nemo murmured to the bridge of the monster's nose, "I will succeed where the others failed. I will bring him to you at eight o'clock tomorrow at that old building downtown."

The man who was Sam's dad had gone, but he'd left behind a sick sort of chuckling. Nemo walked away. If Sam's father followed, he did not know it. And he thought to himself, *Sam is going to be very tall when he grows up.*

He went home and to his bedroom. He needn't have bothered closing the door. No one would notice as he pulled plastic bags from his closet and under his bed and began to sort through the things they would need tomorrow. When he asked his mother where the wrapping paper was, she pointed to the door of the hall closet.

"Please put it back when you're finished with it. Good night."

xiv.

After school, their driver pulled up in an unmarked van. She started talking as soon as they had climbed inside and put their gayly wrapped boxes and backpacks on the floor at their feet.

"Y'all gonna have yourselves a party. That's nice. Seat belts. I don't drive till you're safely belted in your seats."

Click....click.

"I don't mind driving you two, but I'm missing my Bible study, so I'll be streaming it on my phone. You heard right. Bible study. So I don't want no hanky panky back there. You hear?"

She laughed robustly as she pulled away from the curb.

Her Bible study began with the singing of hymns. She sang along.

"I lift my hands, oh oh…"

Beth leaned toward Nemo as far as her seatbelt would permit.

"I have to tell you something."

Nemo was not surprised to see fear in her eyes. He leaned as close to her as he could.

"I stomp my feet in the sanctuary…" their driver sang.

"I already know everything I need to know about you."

"If I'm going to help, I need to get it out of me. Please."

"Only if you really want to." Given what they were about to do, he thought that he understood the gravity of the moment. He did not.

Beth took a deep breath and blew it out slowly.

"I heard grammy say my parents sold me for sex. I don't know what that means."

She wanted – she needed – to scream, but she could not. Her face turned red with the effort to stifle her confusion and her grief. Nemo could not go where she was. The chasm she had opened was too deep for him now. Her anguish, an appalling echo of his own as he'd held his sister and could not will her back to him. He undid his seatbelt and pulled her to him. Her body shivered and quaked in his arms. Her grief poured out of her in bone rattling waves. He thought and thought, wanting desperately to say something to help her. Then his grandmother's voice came unbidden to him.

"Talitha koum," he whispered again and again. *Little lamb, come.*"

Their driver's lesson had begun. *Turn with me to Colossians chapter one verse twenty-seven.*

Breathe.

It took a long time for Beth to fight for and win back her
composure. Oh, so gently, she pushed Nemo away.

"My grammy and grandad are afraid of me."

...the mystery of His will... say it with me.

"Maybe they're afraid because they don't want to think
about what happened to you. Maybe they're afraid because your
dad did something terrible. They can't figure out how they could
have raised someone who did what he did."

"That's what my therapist said. But it's not my fault."

"I know. And you feel like you're in a kind of no man's land
and you can't find your way out."

"How do you know that?"

...Christ in you. The hope of glory.

"Because that's the way I feel. Like nothing matters
anymore. I want to give everybody hell all the time."

"Oh," a sharp intake of breath. "Will it be better when we
stop Sam's dad?"

"It'll be better for Sam. That's enough."

She was breathing normally by the time they reached Sam's
aunt and uncle's home. There was an unmarked police car
already there. Nemo re-buckled his seatbelt. They waited until
their driver pulled the van to the curb and stopped. Only then
did they undo their seatbelts, gather their gift boxes and their
backpacks and wait for their driver to open the door.

xv.

Detective Donnelly was inside. The mood was tense.
Packing boxes crowded both the living room and the foyer.
Sam's uncle greeted them and told them to go upstairs to Sam's
room. His aunt thanked them for coming. Someone would call
them when dinner was ready. They climbed the stairs quietly
and slowly and heard the detective say, "It's not a good idea to
run. We have a better chance of finding him..."

They sat on the floor of Sam's room and opened the boxes.

Both Nemo and Beth had thought to add actual gifts: a stuffed dragon, a baseball, an action figure. These, they set aside. They unpacked a length of knotted rope, latex gloves, a container of charcoal lighter fluid, matches, a wig and a deflated soccer ball.

"What are those for?"

"We need to inflate the soccer ball just enough to put Sam's regular wig on it so it looks like he's asleep in his bed." Nemo handed Sam the soccer ball. "Blow. A little smaller than your head."

They laughed both at Nemo's ingenuity and because they needed to. There was more in their wellsprings than grief.

The floorboards outside Sam's bedroom creaked. There was a gentle knock on his door. Dinner was ready and so were they.

xvi.

Detective Donnelly had gone when they returned downstairs. Sam's aunt had made spaghetti and meatballs. They ate in companionable silence for a long time.

"Tell me about yourself, Nemo."

Nemo smiled across the table at Sam. Then he tapped Beth's foot under the table.

"Nemo looks after us," Beth answered for him. "He tells us jokes and…"

Sam pushed his chair back from the table.

"I'm tired. I'm going to bed. Good night." Picture perfect misery.

He looked at his friends for a long moment.

"Goodbye."

Sam left the room. They could hear him on the stairs.

His aunt stood. His uncle restrained her.

"Let him mourn this loss in peace."

They returned to their meal. Sam's uncle's attempts at quiet joviality were met with equally quiet one-word answers. At last,

his aunt began to clear the table.

xvii.

Their driver held the passenger door open for them. They climbed in.

"Who wants to go home first?"

"My parents are playing bridge at my uncle's. Beth's grandparents decided to go out this evening. Bingo or something. They'll pick her up at my uncle's after."

"Don't nobody tell me nothing."

They travelled a suitable distance in the right direction before Nemo indicated a townhouse with the lights on. He and Beth got out, but he held the door open while Beth took the driver's hand and walked with her to the driver's side door.

"Thank you for helping us visit with our friend. It meant a lot."

She heard the rear passenger door slam closed before she joined Nemo on the sidewalk. Together, they climbed the steps to the front door. Nemo waved *goodbye* to the driver. Beth followed suit. Nemo reached for the doorbell. The van pulled away from the curb.

"We did good," from Sam on the sidewalk.

"Yeah," Nemo and Beth descended from the porch of a stranger's home. "Let's go."

xviii.

The gargoyle-laden tower clock chimed seven in the distance. By Nemo's reckoning, a mistrustful Sam's dad would not arrive for half an hour, hoping to be waiting for them.

The old homeless man met them and let them into the courtyard, helped them pull aside the plywood covering the door that Sam would use to get to the second floor.

"You better make yourself scarce for about an hour," Nemo advised the man. "When we come out, call 911." Nemo handed the man a cellphone. "Don't worry, it's a burner. You can keep it."

If Sam's dad's arrogance won out, he might be late. Nemo hoped he wouldn't risk either alternative and that he would materialize at the stroke of eight.

He did.

"Where is my son?"

Nemo and Beth stood near the roots of the fallen tree. Nemo pointed up along its trunk to the second floor window where Sam was waiting.

"We couldn't stop him. He never climbed a tree before," Beth volunteered, melting against Nemo's side. "I bet you could do it, easy."

He turned to look at her.

"Daddy!" Sam appeared in the second floor window. "Here I am."

Sam 's dad climbed.

"Sammy. My boy. I'm coming. Sammy." That awful voice that he'd meant to be endearing but was monstrous.

While he called out in his sickening sing song, Nemo squirted lighter fluid.

"Imagine that. You climbed all the way up there. What a strong boy you are now. I knew it. I'm sorry I couldn't be with you but with things the way they were... And now..."

Nemo took five matches from the box. He pushed Beth back before he struck them and tossed them at the roots of the tree trunk. The roots lighted with a *whoosh*, a fiery Medusa. Nemo stepped back. The flames climbed as if in pursuit of Sam's dad. The monster, it seemed, did not have eyes in the back of his head or heightened senses.

"Daddy. I'm here. Come get me. Help me down, daddy."

"Sammy, my boy. My dear, dear boy."

The flames were gaining on him, faster than Nemo had anticipated. He had to stop himself from kicking dirt on the flames to slow them down. The flames were hungry. Let them eat.

"Sammy." Plaintive.

He must have felt the heat.

"Sammy!" Furious.

"Here I am daddy."

He climbed faster. His weight was too much for the branches' fragile grip on the side of the building. The upper branches crashed down and stopped well below the window.

"Sammy!"

"Here I am."

Sam had joined his friends near the base of the tree. His father's face contorted with rage. "Sammy Sammy Sammy," he shrieked.

He was screaming when they turned and walked away, his shrieks joining with distant but approaching sirens.

The homeless man pushed open the door for them and held up his burner phone. He was smiling. He saw the burning tree and the devil on it. Worry flashed across his face and disappeared.

"Sam," Nemo said. "There's a police station a couple of blocks in that direction. If you happen to see a police car before you get there, flag it down. Go."

Sam went. He looked back and waved and walked away. Nemo and Beth ducked into the recessed doorway. The sirens were getting louder. The screams of Sam's dad grew hoarser, strained.

"We were never here," Nemo told the homeless man.

"Damn straight," he answered. "Need a ride home?" He tilted his head in the direction of his shopping cart.

"Thank you. Yes."

Nemo lifted Beth into the cart and climbed in behind her. They were covered by a tarp.

"No matter how many cops you see, don't run," Nemo said to the man.

"Damn straight."

xix.

Beth rang the doorbell of her grandparents' townhouse. Her grandmother answered.

"Home already?" she asked, her nose wrinkling, her brows furrowed. "Where do these people live? A garbage dump? Lord, girl. You need a bath." She pulled Beth inside. "Go upstairs and get out of those clothes."

"Could you wash my hair for me?"

A long moment passed. Her grandmother's face softened.

"I'll meet you in the bathroom in a minute. Now, out of those clothes, please."

Beth, her eyes hard and cold, climbed the stairs. And deep in her a fire burned.

xx.

Nemo unlocked his front door, went inside, closed the door and waited for a moment. Then, he took a deep breath.

"I'm home!" he called as loudly as he could.

His parents hurried into the hallway from different directions. He grinned up at them.

"How y'all doing this evening?"

xxi.

Two police officers spoke quietly with Sam's aunt and uncle. When the officers left, they joined Sam at the kitchen table where he stirred a bowl of melted ice cream and wished that Nemo and Beth could have seen him tear the baseball cap and wig from his head before he got into the police car. Before either of his grandparents could say anything, he announced that he wanted to see his mother.

"We've talked about this, Sam. She didn't want you to see her the way she is."

"I saw what he did to her. I need to see her get better."

Epilogue

A man wanted in the brutal attack on his wife has been arrested. He is also suspected in the kidnapping of three young boys. Authorities have provided no further details on the arrest...

In other news, two men suspected in the death of a little girl have been found hogtied in a ditch outside of town. The weapons believed to have been used in the incident were found nearby and have been confirmed...

THE END

About the Wood Shed Writers

The Wood Shed Writers are a collective of writers from many professions and generations, united by a shared passion for creative expression. Based in the Greater Pittsburgh area, they've gathered weekly for years to share their work, offer feedback, and build a space rooted in trust, craft, and laughter.

What began as a private circle of storytelling has grown into something more: a long-held dream to bring their voices to the public. Thus, The Wood Shed Writers publication was born.

How Deep the Sharpened Blade is their first fiction collection, created in the spirit of pulp.

Watch for the next issue later in 2026.

Read more on the web at
www.woodshedwriters.com

Persons of Interest

Beverlee Blair
EDITOR · CONTRIBUTING AUTHOR

Holly Thyen
CONTRIBUTING AUTHOR

Jason Brown
CONTRIBUTING AUTHOR

Lisa McCormack Tajak
CONTRIBUTING AUTHOR · PHOTOGRAPHER

Jeremy Corn
CONTRIBUTING AUTHOR

Susan Iannuzzi
CONTRIBUTING AUTHOR

John Al
CONTRIBUTING AUTHOR

Meghan Snatchko
DESIGNER · CONTRIBUTING AUTHOR · PHOTOGRAPHER